Houdini Dog

Rose Impey
and Jolyne Knox

Collins

Look out for more *Jets* from Collins

For all the little dog lovers
Megan · Sarah · Amy

First published by A & C Black Ltd in 1988
Published by Collins in 1989
10 9 8 7 6
Collins is an imprint of HarperCollins*Publishers*Ltd,
77–85 Fulham Palace Road, Hammersmith, London W6 8JB

ISBN 0 00 673366 2

Text © 1988 Rose Impey
Illustrations © 1988 Jolyne Knox

The author and the illustrator assert the moral right to be identified as the author and the illustrator of the work.
A CIP record for this title is available from the British Library.
Printed and bound in Great Britain by
Caledonian International Book Manufacturing Ltd, Glasgow

Shopping For A Dog

The day we went to get our dog
was the best day of my life.
Me and my sister were soon up

and dressed

and ready to go.

But Mum and Dad
wouldn't wake up.

Come on, Mum.

It's time to go.

'What time is it?'
said Dad.
'The big hand is
on the twelve,'
said my sister,
'and the little hand
is on the seven.'

Seven o'clock?
Seven o'clock!
You've woken us up
at SEVEN O'CLOCK
on a Saturday
to go and buy a dog!
Go away, you pair
of idiots.

'Come back in an hour,' said Mum.
So we did.

'Can we go *now*?' said my sister.
'I must be mad,' said Dad.
But Mum smiled. She was on our side.
'Okay,' she said. 'Let's go shopping.'

We'd never been shopping
for a dog before.

In the car I was writing a list.
'What's that for?' said Dad.
'It's a shopping list,' I said.
'We're only buying one!' said Dad.
'I know that,' I said. 'It's a list of
what to look for.' I wrote:

Our dog must be

'Small,' said Dad.
'Not too small,' said my sister.

I Not too small

'A bitch would be best,' said Mum.
'Then it could have puppies,' I said.
'Make that a dog,' said Dad.

2 A bitch

'I want it to be nice and soft
so I can cuddle up on it,'
said my sister.

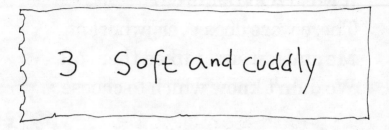

3 Soft and cuddly

'Couldn't we just buy a rug?'
said Dad.
We didn't think that was funny.
'We want a puppy,' I said.
'But puppies mess on the floor,'
said Dad. 'They're worse than babies.'

4 A puppy

'Why don't we just wait and see?'
said Mum.
So that's what we did.

Choosing A Dog

When we got to the dog's home
it was WONDERFUL.
There were dogs everywhere.
Me and my sister liked them all.
We didn't know which to choose.

We couldn't decide.
But in the end we had to.

Mum was tired, my sister was hungry
and Dad looked as if he might
change his mind any minute.
So I said,

Let's have
this one.

And everyone agreed.

It was a little dog – but not too little.
It wasn't a puppy – but it was lively.
It was a bitch with floppy ears
and a tail that wagged all the time.

'Come on,' said Dad. 'That's quite
enough shopping for one day.'

In the car, me and my sister
both wanted to hold the dog.
But she wouldn't keep still.
'What shall we call her?'
I said.

'Trixie?' said Dad. 'That's a wet name.'
'Wanda!' said Mum. 'What kind of a
name is that for a dog?'
'What's wrong with Penny?' I said.
'I shall call her Cuddles,'
said my sister.

'You can't just choose on your own,'
I said. 'We all have to agree on a name.'

But that was the trouble –
we just couldn't agree.

For the rest of the day our dog
got called all sorts of names.
Some of them were a bit silly.

Some of them weren't very nice.

'She *must* have had a name,'
said Mum, 'once upon a time.'
But no one at the dog's home knew it.
We kept trying out different ones
to see if she would answer to any.

But she didn't.

During the day we came up with
lots of new ideas,
but we could never please everyone.

'I think we should wait a few days,'
said Mum, 'until we see what sort
of a character she has.'
'Character?' said Dad. 'It's only a dog.'

'Well, dogs have characters,'
said Mum. 'They have all sorts of odd
little ways. You wait and see.'
Dad didn't like the sound of that.
Then on Friday,' said Mum,
'we can each choose
a name that really suits her,
and we'll decide which is the best.'
And everyone agreed on that.

Mum's Vote

Over the next few days, Mum was
right: our dog turned out to have
lots of funny little ways.
First of all she wouldn't stay in.
The minute the back door was open
she was OFF . . .

. . . racing down the garden path
as fast as her little legs would go.
Her ears flew out at the sides
like a pair of wings.

Right from the start
she tried to escape.

Before we ever let her out into the garden, Dad went round and mended every single gap in the fence.

This is what our garden looks like.

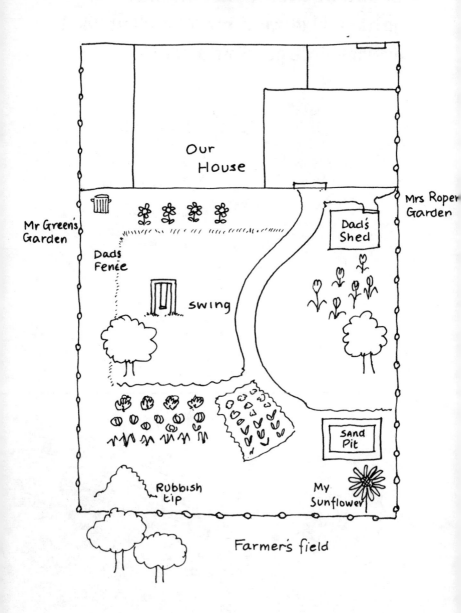

Our House

Mr Green's Garden

Mrs Roper Garden

Dads Fence

Dad's Shed

swing

Rubbish tip

Sand Pit

My Sunflower

Farmer's field

First she escaped at the back.
We found her in the farmer's field,
rolling in some smelly stuff.

That day Dad called her 'Stinker'.
And she was!

Next she escaped on Mr Green's side.
She found a tiny hole,
behind a rose bush.
It looked too small for a cat
to squeeze through.
But our dog got through it.

We found her digging a hole
in the middle of
Mr Green's lawn.
Mr Green called her
a 'Bad dog!'

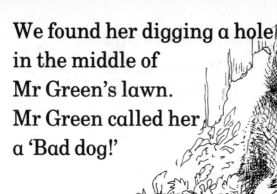

I won't tell you
what Dad called her.

Then she escaped on the other side,
into Mrs Roper's garden.

This time she didn't get
under the fence,
she got *over* it.

We found her eating Toby's food
in Mrs Roper's kitchen.

Toby was hiding under the table,
watching her.
She'd only just had her own tea.
'You greedy pig,' said my sister.

But worst of all, sometimes she got out
at the front.

We tried to keep the front door
closed *all the time*,
in case she got out on the road.

But when
Dad paid
the papers,

or Mum brought
in the milk,

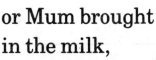

or me and my sister
went to school,

our dog sneaked out.

People were always finding her
and <u>bringing</u> her back.

She was like a little black flash.
'We could call her "Flash",' I said.
'We ought to call her "Houdini",'
said Mum.
'Hoo-what?' said my sister.
'Haven't you ever heard of
Houdini?' said Dad. 'I don't know
what they teach you at school.'

'Houdini was a very famous
"escapologist",' said Mum.
'He used to let people tie him up,

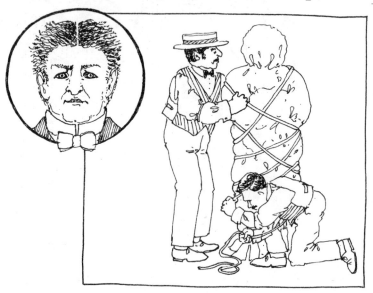

then lock him in a metal box

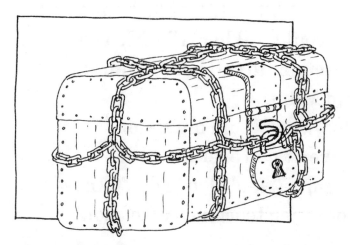

and hang him upside down
from a high building

and he would *still* escape.'

Dad said, 'I bet if we tied that dog
in a sack, and wrapped her up in layers
and layers of brown paper
and put stamps on her
and posted her –
she'd still get free.

She'd probably be sitting on the
front step, waiting to be let in,
before we got back from the post box.'

'Don't be silly,' said my sister.
But I think Dad was right.
She probably would.

Mum thought about it.
'I like it,' she said. 'It suits her.
I think we should call her
"Houdini".'
'Hmmm . . .,' said Dad, 'Not bad.'

But me and my sister didn't think
much of it.
We thought we'd come up with
something better than that.

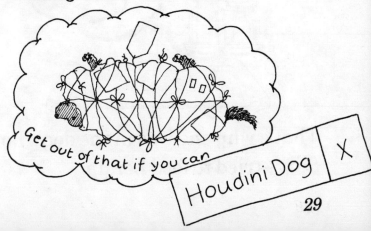

Get out of that if you can

Houdini Dog X

Dad's Vote

Another funny thing about our dog
was she ate everything.
She ate her dog food, of course.
We wanted her to eat that.
But she ate everything else as well.

When we first got her she was thin
and hungry-looking.
She hadn't been fed very much.

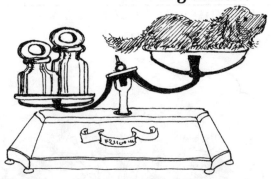

That's why she was in the dog's home.
So we tried to feed her up.

In a morning
we gave her
some milk.

At lunchtime
we gave her
a few dog biscuits.

And at five o'clock
exactly she had
her dinner.

Isn't it time yet?

31

She ate it all in a rush then she sat,
looking up at us, with big sad eyes.
'She looks like Oliver Twist,' said Dad.
'Can't we give her some more?' I said.
'Just a little bit?' said my sister.

'No,' said Mum. 'She mustn't have
too much or she might be sick.'
'She'd better not,' said Dad.
So she lay right in front of the fridge,
hoping that someone might open it.

But Mum and Dad had made some
strict rules about feeding our dog:

No feeding at the table
No eating off our plates
Definitely <u>NO</u> titbits

'We don't want her to get fat, do we?'
said Mum.

But once in a while, when Mum
and Dad weren't looking,
me and my sister gave her

half a biscuit

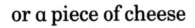

or a piece of cheese

or a Smartie.

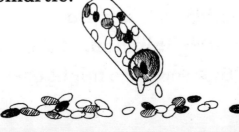

And sometimes we caught Mum
giving her a few scraps,
if she was the one in the kitchen,
doing the cooking.

Shh! Don't tell Dad.

Ah, Mum.

But no matter how much we gave her,
she still wanted more.
She would eat anything.
And I don't just mean food.

In the first week we had our dog
she tried to eat:

1 pencil case

1 hairbrush

2 videos

1 flip-flop

1 phone bill

a Sindy doll's head

half a cushion

a book called 'How To
Train Your Dog'

a box of tissues

a bar of soap

the remote control
for the television

my school project
on the Vikings

my sister's
skipping rope

my mum's glasses

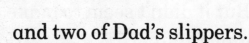

and two of Dad's slippers.

We couldn't leave anything
lying around in the house,
because she would chew a hole in it.

At first Dad got cross.
Then Mum got cross.
Then we all got cross.
But it didn't seem to make
any difference.

'At this rate,' said Dad,
'that dog will have eaten
her way through
the whole house in a month.
We'll end up camping
in the garden.
And then look out . . . she'll probably
eat *us* after that.'

But Mum was worried about her.
'Perhaps she *is* hungry, you know,'
she said.
'Hungry!' said Dad. 'Hungry?
She's nothing but a dustbin on legs.'
And we all had to laugh at that.

Here
Dustbin.

Dad said "Dustbin Dog" suited her
perfectly.
'That's not a proper name,'
said my sister.
But Dad stuck to it.
Well, he wouldn't get my vote.

Dustbin Dog   X

My Sister's Vote

At the beginning, the strangest
thing about our dog was that she
was really quiet.
For four whole days she didn't
make a sound.
She didn't bark or whine or growl.
She didn't seem to have a voice.

Say please...
PLease?

Dad liked it that way.
'At least she's quiet,' he said.
But me and my sister didn't.
We tried to teach her to bark.
We showed her how to do it.

But our dog still didn't speak.

Then, suddenly, when she woke up
on Wednesday morning, she seemed
to decide that this was *her* house.
And from that moment on,
she set out to guard it.
Then she barked *all* the time.

Mostly she barked at cats.
There are lots of cats around us.
Before we had a dog,
Dad said our garden was
like a cat's playing field.
He was always moaning and
trying to get rid of them.

But once we had a dog,
those cats didn't dare
show their faces.

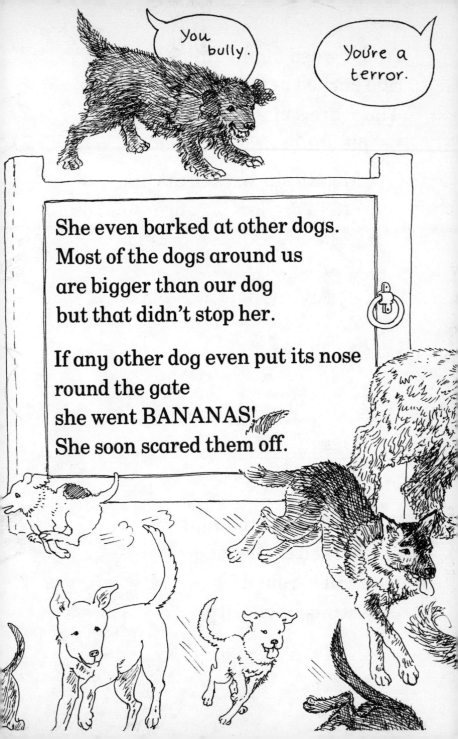

She even barked at other dogs.
Most of the dogs around us
are bigger than our dog
but that didn't stop her.

If any other dog even put its nose
round the gate
she went BANANAS!
She soon scared them off.

And it wasn't only animals.
She barked at people too.
These are some of the dangerous
people she guarded us from:

the plumber   the postman   the newspaper girl   the milkman   Mum's boss

And on Thursday night
she barked at the lady
who called round
collecting for charity.

RSPCA

You're a terror, scaring everyone like that.

She's a bad character.

She's only trying to protect us.

'Cos she loves us.

47

'She just goes out looking for trouble,'
said Dad. 'She's a little demon.'
'She's not a demon,' said my sister.
'She hasn't got any horns.'
'Not yet, she hasn't,' said Dad.
But that gave my sister an idea.

'I like "Demon Dog",' she said.
'That's what I'm going to call her.'

So that only left me
to choose.

Demon Dog X

My Vote

And then it was Friday:
"Naming Our Dog" day.
And I still hadn't chosen.

When we came home
from school,
me and my sister
rushed in as usual
calling for her.

Most days she came running
downstairs or in from the garden.
She did a dance on her back legs
to welcome us home.

49

But that day she didn't come.

We went to find Dad.
He was in his shed.
'Dad, have you seen the dog?' I said.

She was here a minute ago.

We can't find her,' said my sister,
as if she was going to cry.
'Where have you looked?' asked Dad.
Well, we hadn't looked anywhere yet.
So he sent us off to look properly.

We checked all her favourite places:

in the kitchen

under the beds

by the fire

and out in the garden

But she wasn't there.

Just then Mum came home from work.
My sister burst out crying.
'The dog's gone,' she sobbed.
'She's disappeared.'
'Now don't get upset,' said Mum.
'We'll all look. I'm sure she'll turn up.'

'Let's do this properly,' said Dad.
'We'll have a plan.
Mum can look upstairs,
I'll look downstairs,
you two can check the garden.'
'We've looked in the garden,'
said my sister.
'Well, look again,' said Dad.

Plan A

We looked everywhere,
inside every door, behind every bush.
We turned the place upside down.

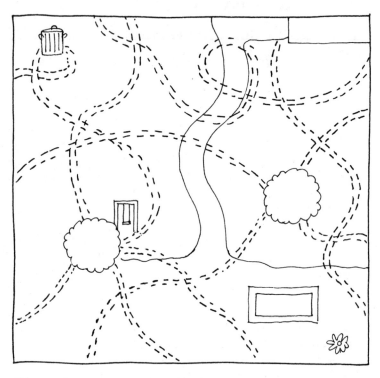

But there was no dog.
Then we knew she'd got out.

So we looked in the farmer's field

and the next-door gardens,

and all down our street.

We asked anybody we saw.
But everybody said, 'No.'

'I think we'd better phone the police,'
said Dad.
'Why? Has she been kidnapped?'
said my sister.
And she began to cry again.

'No, of course not,' said Mum.
'But if anyone finds her they might
take her to the police station.'

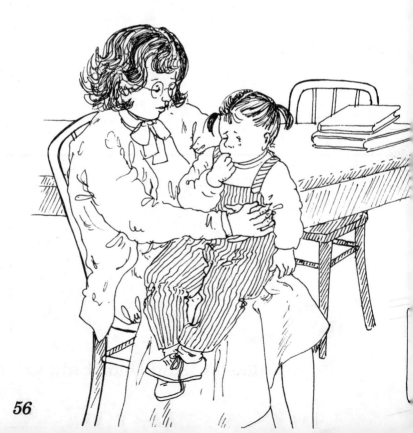

She's got our address on her tag,'
I said. 'But no name.'
We'd had our dog a week
and now we'd lost her.
And she still didn't have a name.
That made *me* want to cry.

'Come on,' said Dad. 'Plan C.'

We drove round for an hour
peering through the car windows,
looking for our missing dog.

But soon it was too dark.
We had to give up and go home.
By now we *all* felt like crying.

We sat there, hoping the phone
would ring,

or someone would knock on the door
to bring her home,

or there would be a little scratch at
the back door.

But there was nothing.

At bedtime our dog was still missing

Come on, time for bed.

'Can't we wait a bit longer?' we said.
'No,' said Mum. 'I'll wake you,
if she turns up.'
'But what if she doesn't?'
said my sister.
Nobody could answer that.
'We could get another dog,
I suppose,' said Dad.
'I don't want another dog,'
said my sister. 'I want our dog.'
And so did I.

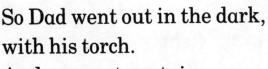

'All right,' said Dad.
'You two go to bed
and I'll go out and
look for her again.'

So Dad went out in the dark,
with his torch.
And we went upstairs.

We were half-way up,
dragging our feet
as slowly as we could,
when suddenly
we heard
Dad call:

'Look who's here.'

Me and my sister ran down those
stairs as fast as we could.
Standing on the kitchen floor
was a very wet, dirty,
scruffy-looking dog.

Ooh!

'She was in the field,'
said Dad.
'As soon as I went out,
I heard her.
She was so tired
I had to lift her
over the fence.'

Me and my sister threw ourselves
on our dog and hugged her
and kissed her
on her little wet nose.
She was really prickly, because
she was covered in holly leaves.
And that's what gave me my idea.

'Now we've got her back,' I said,
'we should give her a name!
And I've got a good name for her.'
Well, really, she'd picked it for herself.

'I think we should call her "Holly",'
I said.

And at last everyone agreed.